Have a Good Day

Philippa Werry

illustrated by Toby Morris

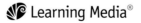 Learning Media®

"Wake up," Seth's mom called.
"It's five after seven.
It's time to get up for school."

"I am getting up," Seth said. "Right now."

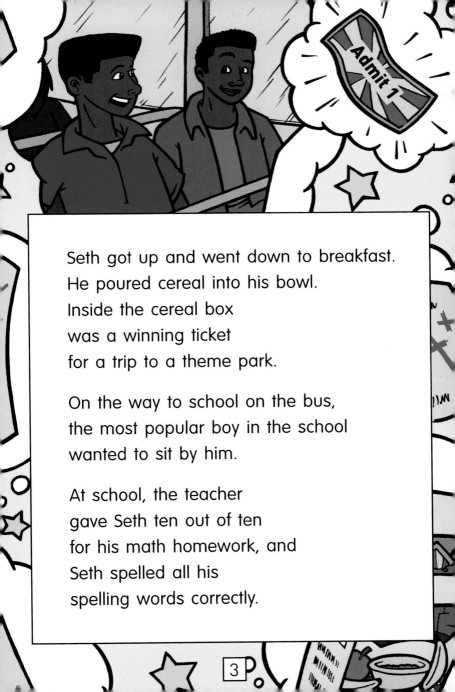

Seth got up and went down to breakfast.
He poured cereal into his bowl.
Inside the cereal box
was a winning ticket
for a trip to a theme park.

On the way to school on the bus,
the most popular boy in the school
wanted to sit by him.

At school, the teacher
gave Seth ten out of ten
for his math homework, and
Seth spelled all his
spelling words correctly.

For school lunch, there were
five different kinds of pizza
and as many doughnuts as Seth wanted.

In the playground, both teams wanted to
pick Seth, and the team he was in won.

After lunch, the teacher read
Seth's book report to the whole class.
She said it was so good
that everyone could have
half an hour of free time.

On the way home on the bus,
the most popular girl in the school
wanted to sit by him.

When Seth got home,
he picked up the mail.
There was a late birthday card
from his uncle with
a fifty-dollar bill inside it.

All his favorite programs were on TV.

Seth's mom cooked his
favorite food for dinner.
He ate so much he snoozed off
in front of the TV.

Then Seth heard his mom calling.
"Wake up! It's ten after seven.
I thought you said you were getting up."

"I am getting up," Seth said. "Right now."
He got up and went down to breakfast.
He poured cereal into his bowl.
Inside the box was a card that said
Seth hadn't won a trip to a theme park.

"Have a good day," his mom called
as he went to meet the school bus.

"I've already had it," Seth said.
"The only problem is –
I was asleep!"